POSTAL™

CREATED BY MATT HAWKINS

VOLUME 4

PUBLISHED BY TOP COW PRODUCTIONS, INC.
LOS ANGELES

POSTAL

CREATED BY MATT HAWKINS

BRYAN HILL
WRITER

ISAAC GOODHART
ARTIST

K. MICHAEL RUSSELL
COLORIST

TROY PETERI
LETTERER

ASHLEY VICTORIA ROBINSON & RYAN CADY
EDITORS

FOR THIS EDITION COVER
LINDA SEJIC

ORIGINAL EDITIONS ED
**ASHLEY VICTORIA R
& RYAN CAD**

BOOK DESIGN & LAYO
TRICIA RAM

For Top Cow Productions, Inc.

Marc Silvestri - *CEO* • Matt Hawkins - *President and COO*

Ashley Victoria Robinson - *Editor* • Elena Salcedo - *Director of Operations*

Henry Barajas - *Operations Coordinator* • Vincent Valentine - *Production Artist*

Dylan Gray - *Marketing Director*

w
for news

IMAGE COMICS, INC.
Robert Kirkman – Chief Operating Officer
Erik Larsen – Chief Financial Officer
Todd McFarlane – President
Marc Silvestri – Chief Executive Officer
Jim Valentino – Vice-President
Eric Stephenson – Publisher
Corey Murphy – Director of Sales
Jeff Boison – Director of Publishing Planning & Book Trade Sales
Jeremy Sullivan – Director of Digital Sales
Kat Salazar – Director of PR & Marketing
Branwyn Bigglestone – Controller
Drew Gill – Art Director
Jonathan Chan – Production Manager
Meredith Wallace – Print Manager
Briah Skelly – Publicist
Sasha Head – Sales & Marketing Production Designer
Randy Okamura – Digital Production Designer
David Brothers – Branding Manager
Olivia Ngai – Content Manager
Addison Duke – Production Artist
Vincent Kukua – Production Artist
Tricia Ramos – Production Artist
Jeff Stang – Direct Market Sales Representative
Emilio Bautista – Digital Sales Associate
Leanna Caunter – Accounting Assistant
Chloe Ramos-Peterson – Library Market Sales Representative

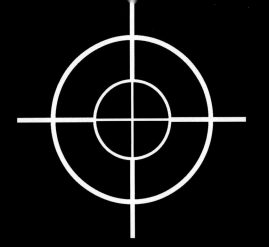

THE TOWN OF *EDEN*, WYOMING, WAS FOUNDED IN SECRET AS AN OFF-THE-GRID HAVEN FOR CRIMINALS, EITHER TO ESTABLISH A NEW IDENTITY OR ESCAPE FROM THE OUTSIDE WORLD.

EDEN WAS FOUNDED BY THE ENIGMATIC AND VIOLENT *ISAAC SHIFFRON*, WHO WAS NEARLY KILLED OVER A DECADE AGO BY HIS THEN-WIFE, *LAURA*, WHO CURRENTLY SERVES AS THE TOWN'S MAYOR.

EDEN, WYOMING

POP

THEIR SON, *MARK*, WHO HAS ASPERGER'S SYNDROME AND WORKS AS THE EDEN POSTMASTER, FUNCTIONS AS A PROBLEM-SOLVER FOR MANY OF THE TOWN'S RESIDENTS...AS WELL AS A SYMBOLIC REPRESENTATION OF EDEN'S FUTURE DAMNATION OR SALVATION.

RECENTLY, EDEN HAS COME UNDER SIEGE BY SEVERAL OUTSIDE THREATS.

THE WELL-MEANING, MAVERICK FBI AGENT *BREMBLE*, WORKING TO UNCOVER THE TRUTH BEHIND THE TOWN...

BUT EVEN WITH BREMBLE OCCUPIED INVESTIGATING EDEN'S PAST, AND MOLLY UNDER LOCK AND KEY, THE TOWN IS ANYTHING BUT SAFE.

THERE'S *VIOLENCE* ON THE HORIZON, AND EDEN'S IN THE CROSSHAIRS...

...AND *MOLLY SCHULTZ*, THE DAUGHTER OF THE FBI DIRECTOR JON SCHULTZ, THE MAN RESPONSIBLE FOR SHIELDING EDEN FROM THE OUTSIDE WORLD.

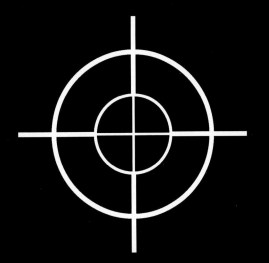

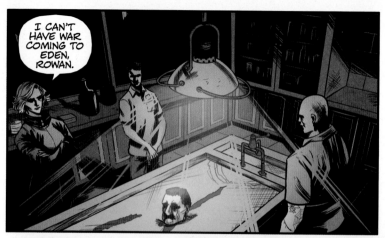

I CAN'T HAVE WAR COMING TO EDEN, ROWAN.

UNDERSTOOD.

THAT FARMHOUSE ON THE OUTSKIRTS OF TOWN. ON THE HILL. ANYONE LIVE THERE?

NO.

THEN I'LL CALL THAT NUMBER AND TELL THE BAD MAN THAT'S WHERE I'LL BE.

GOT A PHONE I CAN USE, MA'AM?

I DO. WHEN YOU'RE FINISHED, I WANT YOU TO COME WITH ME.

MIGHT HAVE SOME HELP FOR YOU.

I HEAR HIS VOICE AND I HAVE TO SLOW MY BREATHING. NO EMOTION FOR HIM. I CAN'T GIVE HIM THAT.

HE TELLS ME WHAT HE DID TO DANNY. HOW LONG IT TOOK.

I STAY QUIET UNTIL HE'S TIRED OF LAUGHING.

THEN I TELL HIM WHERE I'M GOING TO BE AT MIDNIGHT.

NO, ABNER. IT'LL JUST BE ME.

HE ASKS ME IF I'M SURPRISED THAT HE FOUND ME. I TELL HIM NO.

I THINK ABOUT A BLACK BOY BROKEN AND WET ON THE END OF A CHAIN.

I'M NOT SURPRISED YOU FOUND ME, ABNER.

WE ALL GET WHAT WE DESERVE.

THEY'RE GONNA BREED MEN LIKE US OUT. THAT'S THE PLAN. THEY'RE GONNA TURN THIS WHOLE COUNTRY BROWN AND TELL US WE HAVE IT COMING.

JUST LOOK AT THAT NIGGER RIGHT THERE.

NOT A CARE IN THE WORLD.

"JUST LOOK AT HIM.

"LOOK.

"WHEN'S THE LAST TIME YOU FELT LIKE THAT, ROWAN?

"WHEN YOU'RE A WHITE MAN IN AMERICA, YOU HAVE TO MAKE IT RIGHT."

YOUR BROTHER TRIED NOT TO TELL US WHERE YOU WERE.

FOR A LITTLE WHILE.

ARE YOU HERE, TRAITOR?

DO WHAT YOU DO, GENTLEMEN.

BLAM

THE MAN I SHOT WASN'T ABNER. HE WAS SMART ENOUGH TO NOT BE THERE.

BUT THAT MEANS HE'S STILL COMING FOR YOU.

HE SENT YOU A HEAD. WE'RE GONNA SEND SIX OF HIS BACK TO HIM.

I FAILED YOU. I LET YOU DO THIS ALONE. AND I'M SORRY. YOU'RE PART OF EDEN, ROWAN. ONE OF MINE NOW.

I HAVE A LETTER I NEED MARK TO MAIL, TO A WOMAN NAMED MRS. HATTIE JOHN --

MAIL IT WHEN THIS IS DONE. WE HAVE A LOT OF WORK TO DO. FIRST THING?

CALL ABNER. TELL HIM WE'RE READY TO GO TO WAR.

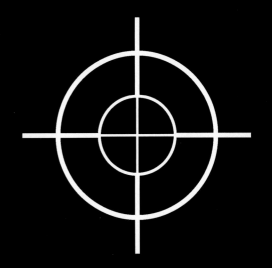

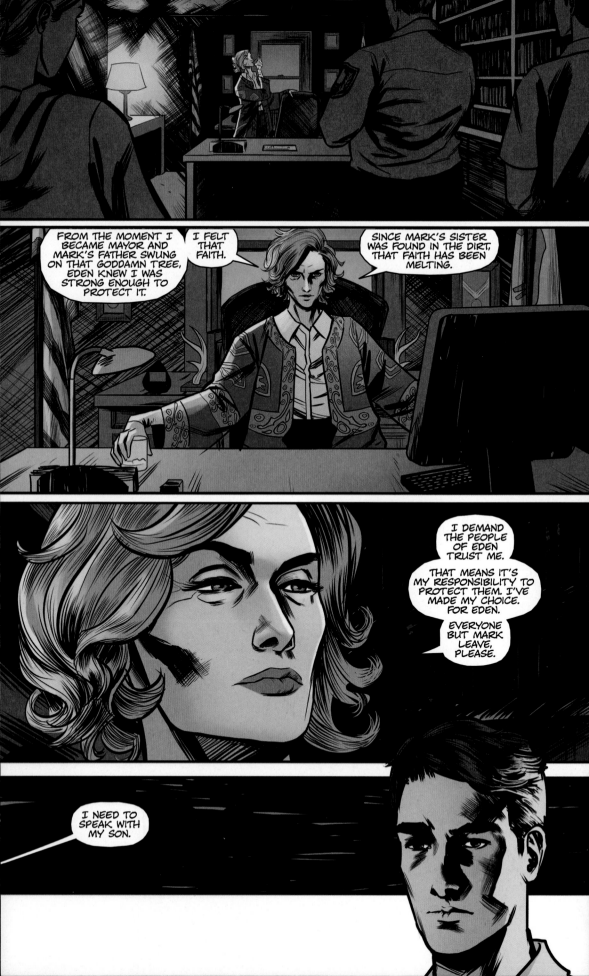

CHAHOKIA, WYOMING.

I NEVER HAD LOVE FOR SYMBOLS. NEVER MUCH MATTERED TO ME.

BUT THE BOYS LIKE TO PLAY WITH THE OLD WAYS.

NO PART OF ME BELIEVES ROWAN SENT THOSE HEADS BACK ON HIS OWN. THAT OLD HORSE IS TOUGH, BUT HE'S NOT THE MIGHTY THOR.

HE'S GOT HELP. THAT HELP IS HIDING HIM.

PUT SOME MONEY ON IT, MICHAEL. USE YOUR BEST COLLEGE WORDS. ASK. BRIBE. FORCE.

THAT TRAITOR'S LEAVING A STINK IN THE AIR. FOLLOW IT.

WHITE POWER!

WHITE POWER!

WHITE POWER!

WHITE POWER!

AND FIND WHERE THIS MOTHERFUCKER BREATHES.

MAYOR SHIFFRON IS GOING TO HELP YOU, ROWAN.

WE SPOKE ABOUT IT. SHE MADE HER CHOICE.

THAT'S RIGHT.

HAVE YOU EATEN, ROWAN?

NOT HUNGRY, MA'AM.

AND I DON'T WANT TO CAUSE OUR TOWN ANY TROUBLE.

'PRECIATE THAT, BUT WHAT THE MAYOR SAYS IS WHAT WE DO.

YES, SIR.

SO WHAT HAPPENS NOW?

EVERY WAR NEEDS AN ARMY --

-- AND WE NEED TO GATHER A COALITION OF THE WILLING.

Carpenter's
SCRAP
SHOP

ABNER.

YOU ONLY SEE ME WHEN THERE'S SOMETHING WRONG.

SO WHAT IS WRONG?

WE'RE AT WAR WITH SOMEONE. HE'S HIDING, BUT I'LL FIND HIM. WHEN I DO, I WANT YOU TO VISIT HIM.

YOU HAVE ROUTINELY REJECTED MY POINT OF VIEW, ABNER. YOU FIND ME ESOTERIC AND IRRELEVANT.

"FUCKING CRAZY" IS WHAT I REMEMBER YOU SAYING. I FOUND THAT HURTFUL.

YOU WANT ME TO BEG, CARPENTER? GET ON MY KNEES?

NO. I DO NOT WANT TO SEE A MAN OF MY BLOOD ON HIS KNEES.

I'VE GOT A POT OF COFFEE I'M WILLING TO SHARE. TELL ME WHAT THREATENS YOU.

IT'S A STATEMENT OF FACT. WYOMING FBI PROTECTS EDEN. EDEN PROTECTS WYOMING FBI. IT'S HOW WE HATE-FUCK EACH OTHER.

SOMETIMES YOU WIND UP BITING THE PILLOW.

JON, I LIVE OUTSIDE OF THE RULES BECAUSE I MAKE THE RULES. IT *FEELS GOOD.* HELP ME END THESE BASTARDS. LIVE LIKE ME ONE TIME. BE THE MAN I KNOW YOU CAN BE.

I KNOW WHERE ABNER KEEPS HIS HEROIN. I DON'T HAVE A WARRANT TO GET IT, BUT I KNOW WHERE IT IS. I'LL NEED A COUPLE OF WEEKS TO GET IT DONE.

IN THIS HYPOTHETICAL REALITY WHERE I DO THIS...WHERE DO I PUT THIS HEROIN TO MAKE YOUR LITTLE TRAP?

TELL ME WHEN IT'S DONE AND I'LL GET BACK TO YOU.

LAURA. *WAIT.*

WHEN HAVE YOU EVER FELT THIS POWERFUL?

...OH...

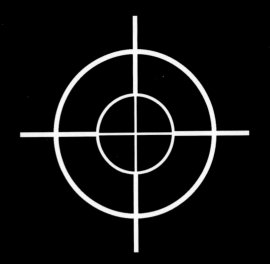

SKREEE

SHRAAAANK

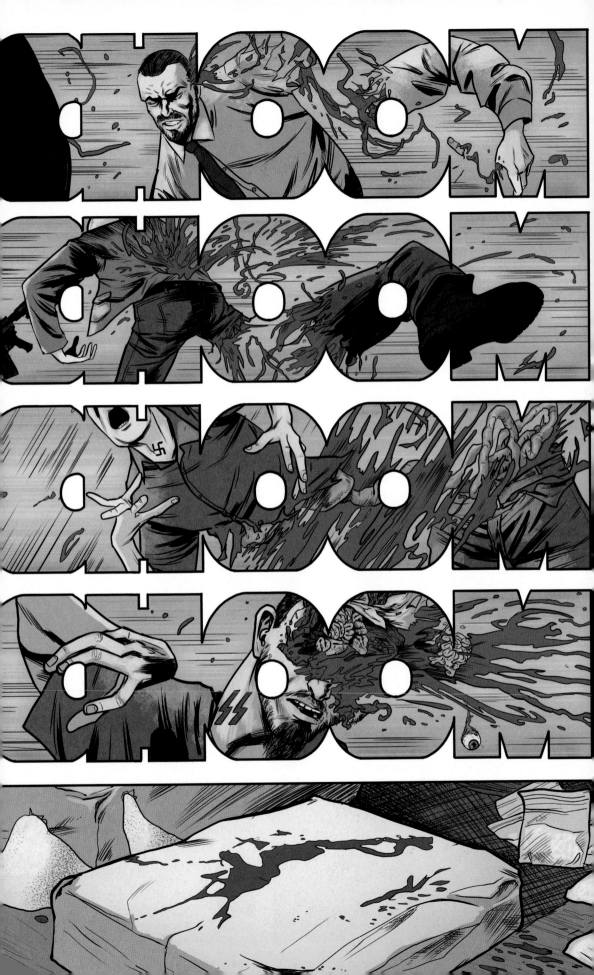

THNK

BWOOM

"WE'LL GET THE RESULTS BACK SOON, LAURA."

EDEN MEDICAL CENTER

EDEN MEDICAL CENTER

IN THE MEANTIME, I SUGGEST REDUCING YOUR STRESS. TAKE IT EASY FOR A BIT.

TAKE IT EASY.

I'LL DO MY BEST.

MAY I ASK YOU A PERSONAL QUESTION, LAURA?

YOU'RE MY DOCTOR. THAT'S ALL YOU ASK.

HAVE YOU CONSIDERED WHO WILL TAKE CHARGE OF THE TOWN WHEN YOU RETIRE?

I DON'T CONSIDER RETIREMENT.

EVERY KINGDOM NEEDS A LINE OF SUCCESSION. AND YOUR SUBJECTS DON'T HAVE FAITH IN THE PRINCE.

IF ANYONE HAS A PROBLEM WITH MY BOY, THEY CAN FEEL FREE TO TALK TO ME ABOUT IT.

BUT THEY SHOULD BE VERY CAREFUL WHAT THEY SAY.

I'M NOT GETTING WEAKER, DOCTOR. I'M GETTING TIRED.

EDEN SURVIVES BECAUSE THEY FEAR THAT ANGER, LAURA.

NO ONE FEARS YOUR SON.

IF PEOPLE BELIEVE YOU'RE GETTING WEAKER, THEY'LL PROVE THAT TO YOU.

I SINCERELY HOPE I DON'T HAVE TO SHOW YOU ALL THE DIFFERENCE BETWEEN THE TWO.

CALL ME WITH THE TEST RESULTS. THE ONLY PEOPLE WHO KNOW ABOUT THIS ARE YOU AND MY SON. MY SON WON'T TELL ANYONE.

SO IF I HEAR ANYONE IN EDEN MENTION MY HEALTH, I'LL VISIT YOU FIRST. ARE WE CLEAR?

COMPLETELY. GET SOME SLEEP. DRINK MORE WATER.

AND REMEMBER YOU'RE MORTAL LIKE EVERYONE ELSE.

I HAVE A MESSAGE FOR ABNER.

WHO IS THIS?

WE HAVE YOUR NARCOTICS. BASED ON THE MONETARY VALUE THEY HAVE IN ILLEGAL SALES, I BELIEVE YOU WOULD LIKE TO HAVE THOSE NARCOTICS BACK IN YOUR POSSESSION.

PLEASE DON'T RESPOND UNTIL I AM FINISHED.

IF YOU WOULD LIKE TO RETRIEVE YOUR NARCOTICS, YOU WILL GET ANOTHER PHONE CALL WITH A TIME AND LOCATION TO COLLECT THEM, BUT YOU WILL HAVE TO DO SO IN PERSON.

IF YOU DO NOT DO SO IN PERSON, YOUR NARCOTICS WILL BE DESTROYED. I BELIEVE THE APPROXIMATE MONETARY LOSS OF THAT WOULD BE OVER A MILLION DOLLARS. I AM FINISHED. YOU CAN RESPOND NOW.

WHO IS THIS? WHO DO YOU WORK FOR?

THE POST OFFICE.

BECAUSE IT'S NICE TO KNOW WHAT MY LIFE IS WORTH.

YOU WANT TO HATE ME? HATE ME. BUT I DON'T HAVE TO LET YOU MAKE ME FEEL IT.

GO HOME, CURTIS.

WHEN YOU WERE DRAGGING HIM. COULD YOU HEAR HIM?

UNTIL HE STOPPED MAKING SOUNDS.

HOW'D YOU FEEL ABOUT IT?

FUCK GOD.

WHATEVER MARK WANTS TO DO, I'M IN.

WHY?

HE'S *DONE*, MAGGIE. HE WANTS THEM TO KILL HIM.

AND I DON'T WANT HIM TO GET WHAT HE WANTS.

GOOD MORNING, ABNER.

THEY WANT ME TO BE THERE. THIS IS ABOUT KILLING ME, CARPENTER.

THEN YOU WILL BE THERE.

BECAUSE WE ARE NOT COWARDS. WE ARE WARRIORS.

YOU SHOULD BE ASHAMED OF THE FEAR IN YOUR VOICE. YOU SHOULD TRUST THE *POWER* OF YOUR BLOOD.

I'LL GIVE YOU THE LOCATION WHEN THEY SEND IT. JUST HELP ME KILL THEM. LECTURE ME LATER.

I HAVE TO MAKE BREAKFAST FOR LUCY.

Call Ende

BLEE

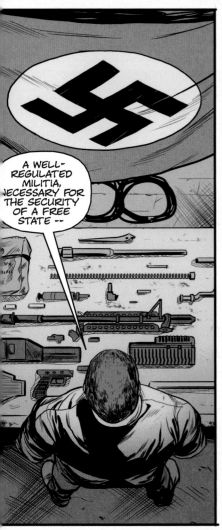

A WELL-REGULATED MILITIA, NECESSARY FOR THE SECURITY OF A FREE STATE --

THE RIGHT OF PEOPLE TO KEEP AND BEAR ARMS --

CLICK

SHALL NOT BE INFRINGED.

WE ARE THE RACE THAT LEADS THE WORLD. WE ARE WARRIORS AGAINST CHAOS. WE WILL NOT STAND SILENT AS SOME WAGE BATTLE AGAINST US. WE WILL TAKE THE CHARGE OF THE SENTINEL.

WHITE POWER.

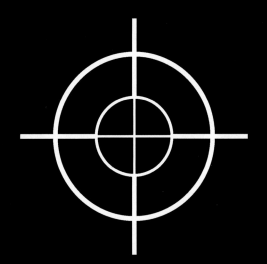

OKAY.

TRUST MAGGIE. SHE'S THE STRONGEST OF THEM.

ROWAN AND CURTIS ARE WILLING, BUT MAGGIE HAS MORE OF THE DEVIL IN HER. KEEP HER CLOSE TO YOU. ROWAN IS A BROKEN MAN WHO WANTS TO DIE. CURTIS IS A MAN WITH SOMETHING TO PROVE. USE THAT.

SACRIFICE THEM BOTH IF YOU HAVE TO. THEY'RE NOT PEOPLE. THEY'RE PAWNS. THAT'S HOW YOU PLAY THE BOARD. DO YOU UNDERSTAND?

YES. I UNDERSTAND.

MAGGIE'S YOUR QUEEN ON THE BOARD. YOU'RE THE KING. THE GAME ENDS IF YOU DIE.

THE KING MUST BE WILLING TO SACRIFICE HER IF HE NEEDS TO. I KNOW YOU LOVE HER.

BUT YOU CAN'T LOVE HER TONIGHT. DO YOU UNDERSTAND?

YES.

IS THERE ANYTHING ELSE YOU NEED TO TELL ME?

SURVIVE.

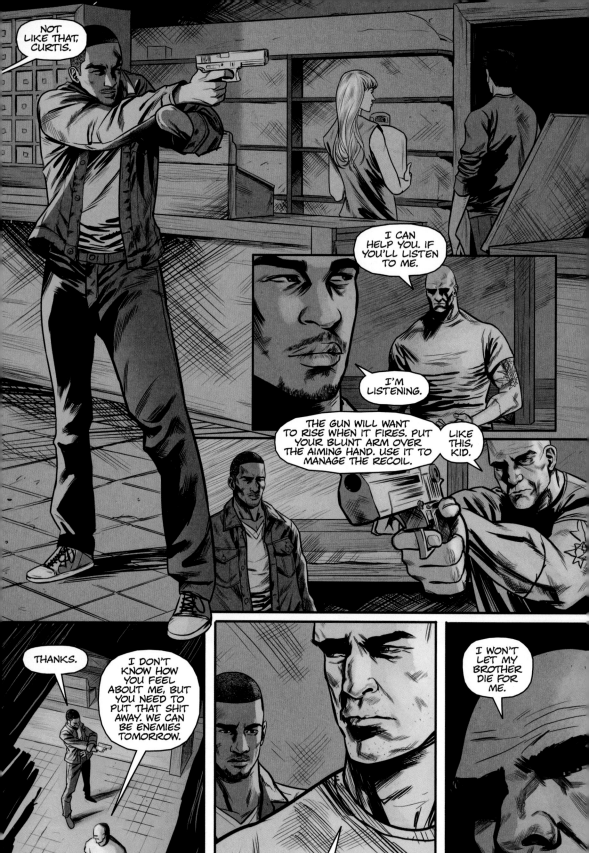

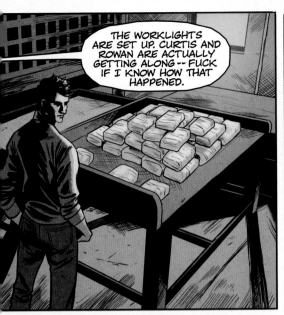

THE WORKLIGHTS ARE SET UP. CURTIS AND ROWAN ARE ACTUALLY GETTING ALONG -- FUCK IF I KNOW HOW THAT HAPPENED.

YOU'RE THINKING. I WOULD FEEL A WHOLE LOT BETTER IF I KNEW WHAT YOU WERE THINKING ABOUT.

IT'S NOT A PLEASANT THING TO SAY. IT'S SOMETHING THAT MIGHT HURT YOU.

SECRETS HURT ME MORE.

MY MOTHER TOLD ME I NEEDED TO BE ABLE TO SACRIFICE YOU. SHE SAID I NEEDED TO BE WILLING TO LET YOU DIE.

DADDY, WHO'S THAT MAN BY THE TRUCK?

NO ONE YOU EVER NEED TO MEET, ANGEL.

DADDY HAS TO GO WITH HIM. I'LL BE BACK IN THE MORNING. BE GOOD FOR MOMMY.

DON'T FORGET TO SAY YOUR PRAYERS BEFORE BED.

I'M READY, CARPENTER.

HARDLY, BROTHER. BUT YOU CAN DRIVE US THERE.

TAKE THE RIDE TIME TO GET YOUR MIND READY.

THIS IS WHITE MAN'S WORK.

CARPENTER-- WHAT THE FUCK?!

YOU'RE THE TYPE WHO LIKES TO RUN.

THERE'S NO RUNNING TONIGHT.

WHEN I COME BACK OUT, YOU'LL KNOW IT'S DONE.

OLLY, OLLY.

MARK! STAY BEHIND ME!

AND MAGGIE'S THE QUEEN.

HOLD IT...LIKE THIS?

JUST... LIKE... THAT.

WE SURVIVED.

EDEN, WYOMING. 24 HOURS LATER.

"I MAILED YOUR LETTER, ROWAN. AND I CHECKED TO MAKE SURE MRS. HATTIE JACKSON RECEIVED IT.

"MY MOTHER FOUND SOMEONE TO BUY THOSE NARCOTICS. BECAUSE OF THE CIRCUMSTANCES, THEY HAD TO BE SOLD AT 30% OF THEIR MARKET VALUE.

"APPROXIMATELY THAT VALUE WAS TWO HUNDRED AND SIXTY-FIVE THOUSAND DOLLARS."

I SENT THAT WITH THE LETTER. I ASSUMED THAT WOULD BE ALL RIGHT WITH YOU.

YOU BOTH SHOULD REST.

ROWAN.

YEAH, KID.

WE'RE STILL BROTHERS.

END

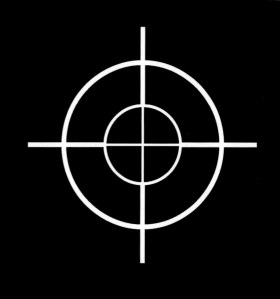

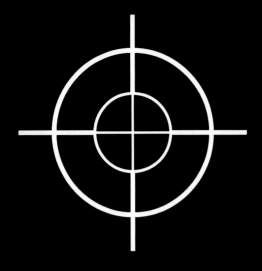

MAIL CALL

HEY THERE, POSTAL FANS!

Thanks so much for picking up this volume of *Postal*. It means so much to all of us here at Top Cow, and, as always, we ask that if you enjoyed this volume, please recommend it to your friends and put in on your pull list at your local comic shop! We love making this book, and we hope you love reading it, and we hope to keep putting it out for many issues to come!

First, let's give a big welcome to new series colorist **K. Michael Russell** — this dude is one of the greats, and if his first issue is any indication, he's bringing out the big guns for this exciting new story arc, a plot that **Bryan Hill** has been waiting to tell since the first issue of the series, as savvier readers will remember Rowan entering the town way back in issue #1.

In case you've forgotten, here's that fateful first meeting:

But this storyline is also about some difficult topics, as Bryan discussed on Facebook:

"Social issues in comic books can be a mixed bag. Often they're presented in a myopic way, usually just preaching to the choir of people on one side of the issue. The work is well intentioned, but usually shallow. The naming of monsters. The scorning of monsters. The pride of being righteous.

That's easy. I've never been interested in what's easy.

[This arc] features a member of the fictional town of Eden, a former member of the Aryan Brotherhood, the cold patience of karma and the price of redemption.

It's NOT a diatribe or an oversimplification of cultural conflict in America. It's an examination of the roots of anger and fear that sprout into these movements. As we see the rise of populism and nativism in the world around us, my hope is it's a unflinching exploration of these issues, framed in a DAMN COOL CRIME STORY about a town full of fugitives trying on the skin of living new lives."

Have something to say about the new arc? We'd love to hear from you! Send your letters for the *Postal* team to **fanmail@topcow.com** (and if you want, mark them "**Okay to Print**," and we'll put them here for all to see)! Who knows, **Postmaster Mark** might even take a look at it himself.

MAIL CALL

If you've been following this book since *Volume 1*, you know that writer **Bryan Hill** can be a pretty insightful guy — it's safe to say that we're fans of his. If you want more of that insight, you can actually read Bryan in conversation with some other smart comic book people, and read interviews and op-eds conducted by him on at **comicsbeat.com** — there's one up there now with Jonathan Hickman and another with Greg Pak that'll knock your socks off.

But we know that comics is what you care about, which is why we want you to check out *Romulus* — **Bryan Hill** and **Nelson Blake II's** new creator-owned series, out now from Top Cow. Dig on this solicit text, and check out some art below:

"Our world isn't free. All of us, for generations, have lived under the secret control of The Ancient Order of Romulus. One young woman, raised by them, trained by them, betrayed by them, must push through her fear to take a stand against the silent evil that masters our world. Her name is Ashlar, and her war begins with the brutal first chapter of the new Image series ROMULUS, from writer BRYAN HILL (POSTAL) and artist NELSON BLAKE II (MAGDELENA)."

Pretty cool, right? But why should we leave you hanging with just one art preview?

Flip to the end of this book to read a quick preview of *Eden's Fall #1*, the first of a three-issue miniseries taking place in Eden, and featuring characters **from this book** — along with a few friends from *Think Tank* and *The Tithe*. It's in stores now, and co-written by **Bryan Hill** and **Matt Hawkins** — check it out!

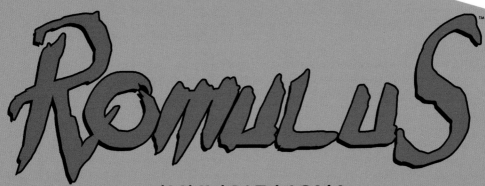

BRYAN HILL
NELSON BLAKE II

ROMULUS

AVAILABLE NOW

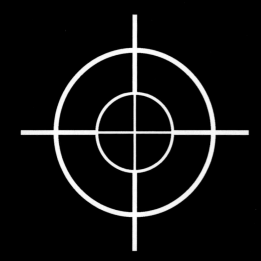

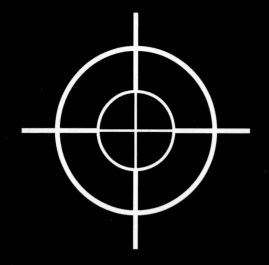

POSTAL #13
COVER A
LINDA SEJIC

POSTAL #13   COVER B   ISAAC GOODHART & K. MICHAEL RUSSELL

POSTAL #14
COVER A
LINDA SEJIC

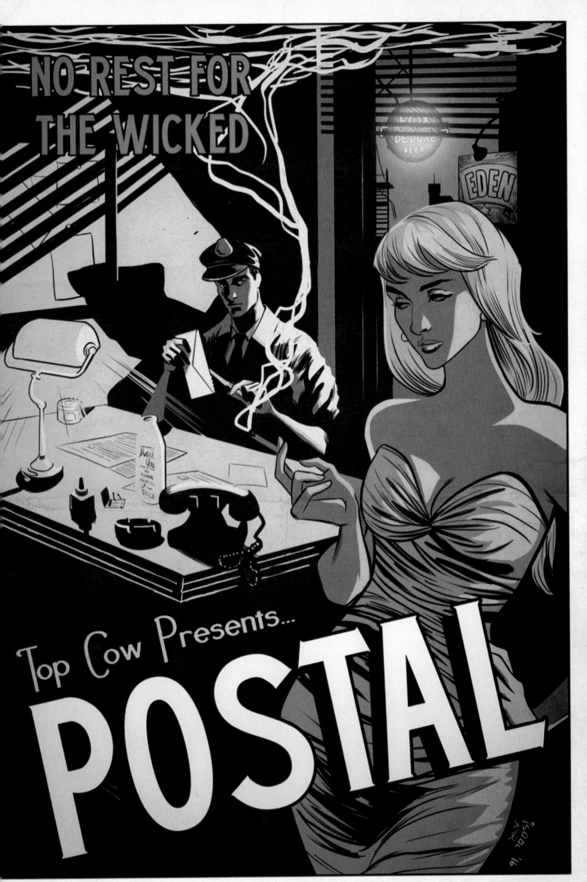

POSTAL #15
COVER A
LINDA SEJIC

POSTAL

ISSUE 15

POSTAL #15
Cover B
Isaac Goodhart &
K. Michael Russell

BRYAN
HILL

ISAAC
GOODHART

K. MICHAEL
RUSSELL

MATT
HAWKINS

TOP COW PRODUCTIONS INC PRESENTS AN EDEN-VERSE COMIC BOOK PRODUCTION CREATED BY MATT HAWKINS
WRITTEN BY BRYAN HILL DRAWN BY ISAAC GOODHART COLORED BY K. MICHAEL RUSSELL LETTERED BY TROY PETERI
EDITED BY RYAN CADY AND ASHLEY VICTORIA ROBINSON PRODUCED BY TRICIA RAMOS

POSTAL #16
COVER A
LINDA SEJIC

BRYAN
HILL

ISAAC
GOODHART

K. MICHAEL
RUSSELL

MATT
HAWKINS

THESE CRIMINALS WANT JUSTICE

POSTAL

TOP COW PRODUCTIONS INC. PRESENTS AN EDEN-VERSE COMIC BOOK PRODUCTION
WRITTEN BY BRYAN HILL DRAWN BY ISAAC GOODHART COLORED BY K. MICHAEL RUSSELL
LETTERED BY TROY PETERI EDITED BY ASHLEY VICTORIA ROBINSON PRODUCED BY TRICIA RAMOS

Postal #16 Cover B Isaac Goodhart & K. Michael Russell

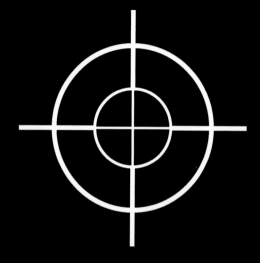

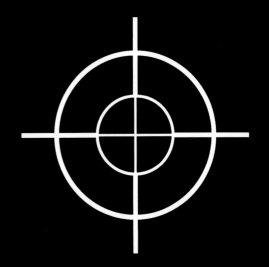

SAM'S IN.

WE'RE A GO.

DID YOU FIX IT?

ALL OF IT.

RUN ME THROUGH THE COVER.

THINGS GO WRONG IN LADY-LAND? SAM'S GOT A TEMPER, BUT ALL YOU NEED TO DO IS--

STOP TALKING TO ME, LOREN. LIKE *FOREVER.*

SUBJECT CHANGED--

--THE EDEN CONTACT WANTS A NIGHT TRANSFER. TWO A.M. I GOT A RED-EYE TICKET FOR YOU UNDER THE FALSE NAME. I'LL BE IN WYOMING, BUT THE PICKUP HAS TO BE YOU ALONE. THEY SMELL US, AND THEY'LL WALK-- AND OUR WINDOW *CLOSES.*

YOU CAN STILL SAY NO TO THIS, JIMMY. WE'LL STILL BE GOOD IF YOU SAY NO.

DWAYNE. LET'S FIND HIM.

CONTINUED IN EDEN'S FALL #1, IN STORES NOW!

MEET THE CREATORS

MATT HAWKINS

A veteran of the initial Image Comics launch, Matt started his career in comic book publishing in 1993 and has been working with Image as a creator, writer, and executive for over twenty years. President/COO of Top Cow since 1998, Matt has created and written over thirty new franchises for Top Cow and Image including *Think Tank, Necromancer, VICE, Lady Pendragon,* and *Aphrodite IX* as well as handling the company's business affairs.

BRYAN HILL

Writes comics, writes movies, and makes films. He lives and works in Los Angeles. @bryanedwardhill | Instagram/bryanehill

ISAAC GOODHART

A life-long comics fan, Isaac graduated from the School of Visual Arts in New York in 2010. In 2014, he was one of the winners for Top Cow's annual talent hunt. He currently lives in Los Angeles where he storyboards and draws comics.

K. MICHAEL RUSSELL

Michael has been working as a comic book color artist since 2011. His credits include the upcoming Image series *Glitterbomb* with *Wayward* & *Thunderbolts* writer Jim Zub, *Hack/Slash*, *Judge Dredd*, and the Eisner and Harvey-nominated *In the Dark: A Horror Anthology*. He launched an online comic book coloring course in 2014 at ColoringComics.com and maintains a YouTube channel dedicated to coloring tutorials. He lives on the coast in Long Beach, Mississippi, with his wife of sixteen years, Tina. They have two cats. One is a jerk. @kmichaelrussell

TROY PETERI

Starting his career at Comicraft, Troy Peteri lettered titles such as *Iron Man*, *Wolverine*, and *Amazing Spider-Man*, among many others. He's been lettering roughly 97% of all Top Cow titles since 2005. In addition to Top Cow, he currently letters comics from multiple publishers and websites, such as Image Comics, Dynamite, and Archaia. He (along with co-writer Tom Martin and artist Dave Lanphear) is currently writing (and lettering) *Tales of Equinox*, a webcomic of his own creation for www.Thrillbent.com. (Once again, www.Thrillbent.com.) He's still bitter about no longer lettering *The Darkness* and wants it back on stands immediately.